Splat

Fishy Tales

For Owen. May you have many fishy tales to tell.

–R.S.

www.robscotton.com

First published by HarperFestival, an imprint of HarperCollins Publishers, USA, in 2012
First published in paperback in Great Britain by HarperCollins Children's Books in 2013

1 3 5 7 9 10 8 6 4 2
ISBN: 978-0-00-751988-0

HarperCollins Children's Books is a division of HarperCollins Publishers Ltd.

A CIP catalogue record for this title is available from the British Library.

Typography by Rick Farley

Visit our website at: www.harpercollins.co.uk

Printed in China

Splat Fishy Tales

Created by

Rob Scotton

HarperCollins *Children's Books*

Splat and his class were going on a trip to the aquarium.

AQUARIUM
SPIKE

Splat sat on the bus. He wished he was sitting next to Kitten.

When they arrived at the aquarium, Mrs Wimpydimple made an announcement: "Only *look* at the sea creatures – no touching!" she said.

"And no eating them, either!"

As the cats headed to the first tank, Splat knew he really wanted to impress Kitten. But how?

As soon as he saw the jellyfish, he had an idea. . .

"Did you know that jellyfish are made from strawberry jelly?" said Splat.

"That's not right," said Spike.

Splat's tail wiggled worriedly. Was Spike right?
But Splat wasn't going to give up that easily.

The class moved on to the sea dragon tank.

VISITOR
PLANK
VISITOR
Max
AQUARIUM

"Did you know that sea dragons are really tiny dragons that shoot out fire?" Splat said.

"That's not right," said Spike.

"The water puts out the fire too quickly for you to see it," Splat insisted. He felt like a real expert now.

At the tropical reef tank, Splat spotted a cowfish.
"Cowfish are actually tiny little cows," he declared.

“That’s not right,” said Spike.

“Then why are they called that?” asked Splat.

Splat didn't wait for an answer.
He could see Kitten smiling at him.
His plan was working!

Splat skipped happily over to the next tank,

when suddenly he tripped and. . .

SPLAT!

Spike laughed. "Splat finally got one right. That really is a catfish tank now!"

As Splat dried off, Kitten thanked him for making the aquarium so interesting
"At least you didn't fall in the dogfish tank!" she said with a giggle.

More fantastic books by Rob Scotton

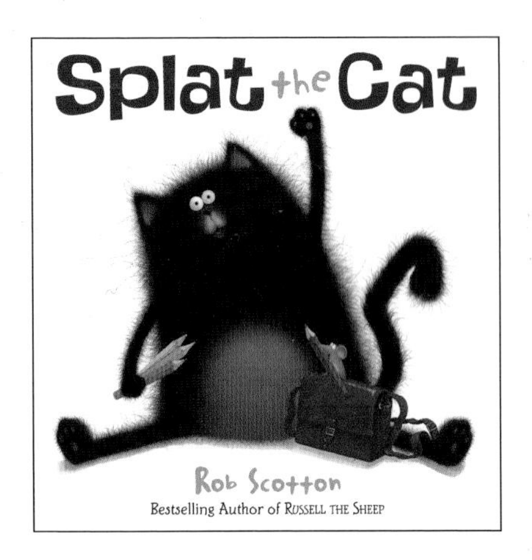

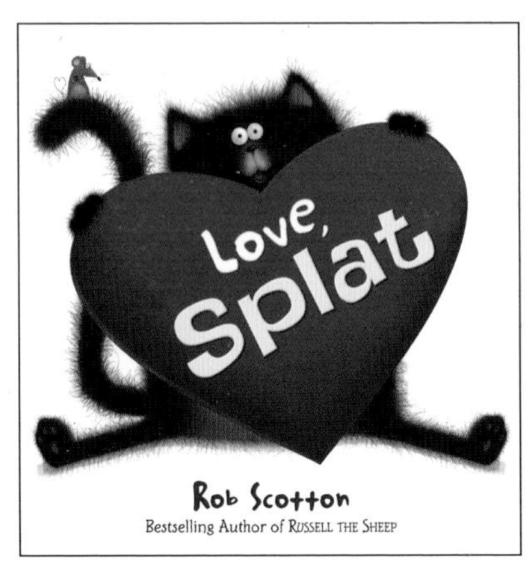

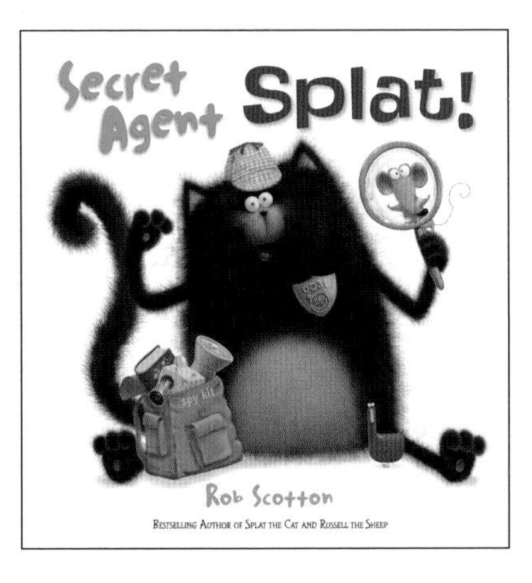